Just Ducky
Kathy Mallat

Walker & Company
New York

For Erin,

As you venture away from home,

Remember you're never really alone.

First published in the United States of America in 2002 by Walker Publishing Company, Inc.
Published simultaneously in Canada by Fitzhenry and Whiteside, Markham, Ontario L3R 4T8

For information about permission to reproduce selections from this book, write to
Permissions, Walker & Company, 435 Hudson Street, New York, New York 10014

Library of Congress Cataloging-in-Publication Data

Mallat, Kathy.
Just ducky / Kathy Mallat
p. cm.
Summary: A lonely little duck looks into the water and finally finds someone to play with.
ISBN 0-8027-8824-6   —   ISBN 0-8027-8825-4 (rein)
[1. Ducks—Fiction. 2. Play—Fiction. 3. Friendship—Fiction. 4. Reflection (Optics)—Fiction.]
I. Title.
PZ7.M29455 Ju 2001
[E]–dc21   2001056841

The illustrations were made on 16-ply Crescent illustration board using Prismacolor
permanent markers, Prismacolor colored pencils, Sakura oil pastels, and Liquitex
acrylic paint.

Book design by Bruce McMillan

Visit Walker & Company at www.walkerbooks.com
and Kathy Mallat at www.kathymallat.com

Printed in Hong Kong

10 9 8 7 6 5 4 3 2 1

JJ
MALLAT
KATHY

While Mama's enjoying this just ducky day,

Ducky is looking for friends to come play.

So he quacks and squawks calling Bee to come play,
but Bee is too busy bizz-buzzing away.

So he quacks and squawks calling Mouse to come play,
but Mouse is too busy dash-darting away.

So he quacks and squawks calling Frog to come play,
but Frog is too busy hip-hopping away.

With no one around, Ducky's feeling quite blue.

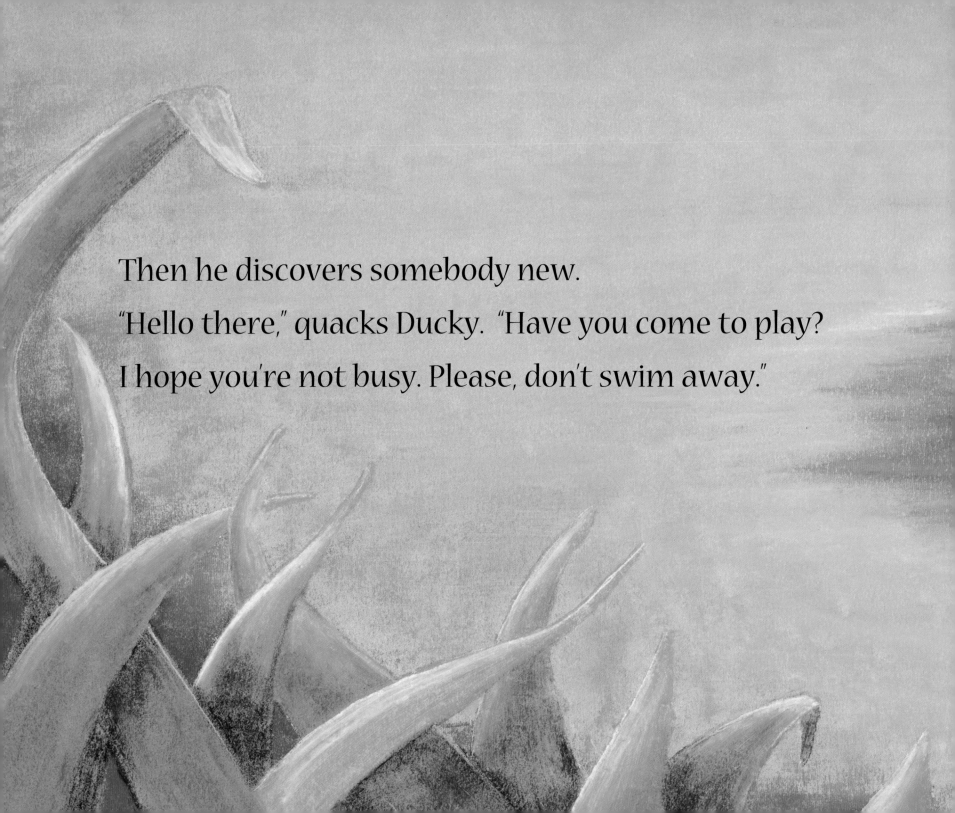

Then he discovers somebody new.

"Hello there," quacks Ducky. "Have you come to play?

I hope you're not busy. Please, don't swim away."

"Let's play," squawks Ducky.

"Can you float on your back?

Can you blow bubbles?

Can you sing a loud quack?"

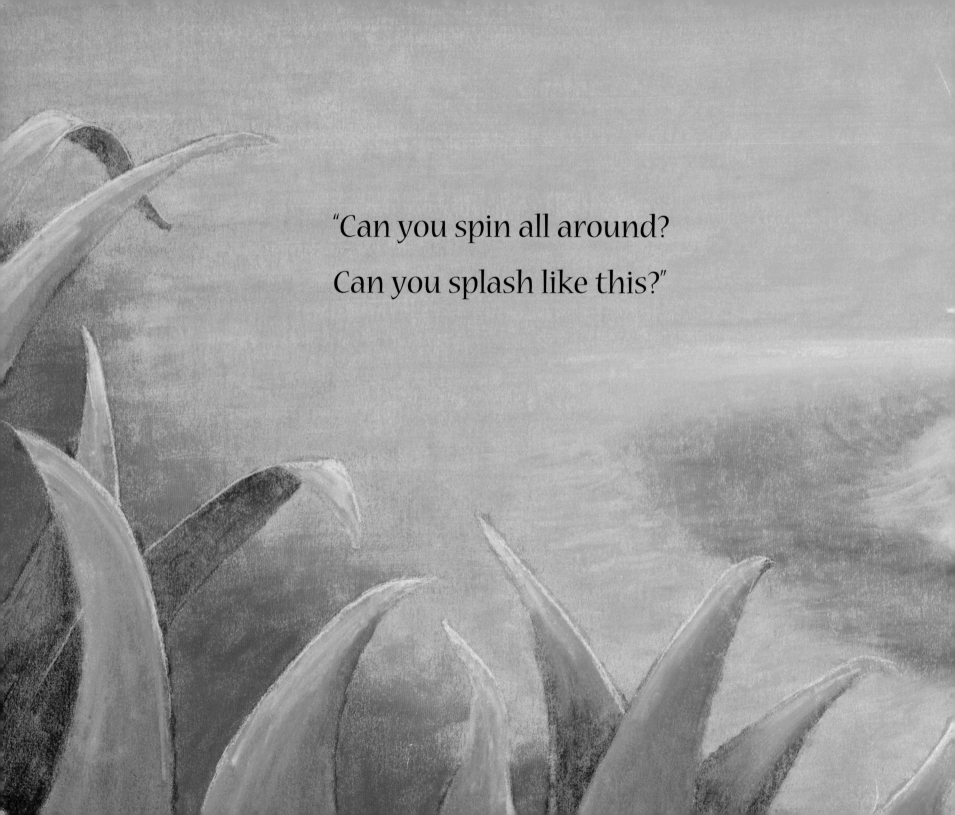

"Can you spin all around?

Can you splash like this?"

"Can you dunk upside down?

Can you swim like a fish?"

Ducky's delighted that his friend stays to play.

"What a warm and wonderful, just ducky day."

They play and splish-splash till the day is all done.

"Mama, being just Ducky was just ducky fun."